M000159623

This book belongs to

_____

For my children Kiana, Kinsley and Landon.

May you continue to find shooting stars and make beautiful wishes.

Copyright © 2020 Sarina Siebenaler
All rights reserved. No part of this publication may be reproduced, distributed, or transmitted in any form or by any means, including photocopying, recording, or other electronic or mechanical methods, without the prior written permission of the publisher, except in the case of brief quotations embodied in critical reviews and certain other non-commercial uses permitted by copyright law.
For permission requests contact: books@sarinasiebenaler.com

ISBN: 978-1-7351996-0-3 (Hardback)
978-1-7351996-1-0 (Paperback)
978-1-7351996-2-7 (Ebook)

Library of Congress Control Number: 2020917302

Illustrations by Gabby Correia
Book Design by Praise Saflor

First printing edition 2020

Colors on the Spectrum

www.sarinasiebenaler.com

Do NOT WiSH FOR A PET OSTRICH!

By Sarina Siebenaler

Illustrated by Gabby Correia

My parents once said I could pick out a pet,
but it had to be one that I'll never regret.

Once Sally picked wrong when she chose a cute pup.
Now she can't find a shoe that has not been chewed up.

And Tom has a cat that he says is too lazy. Just snoozing all day, making everyone crazy.

My teacher's pet parrot at first seemed so fun.
But it chatters so much that she gets nothing done.

"EUREKA!" I shouted.

"I know what I'll get!
An OSTRICH will be the
best pet I can get!"

So, I wished on a star shooting off in the night.
I wished for an ostrich with all of my might.

Oh star, shining star, make my wishes come true,
please send me a bird like the ones in the zoo.

And please will you give him a long, skinny neck.
And also, please give him a beak that will peck.

Then...

Asleep I went...

Woke up to check...

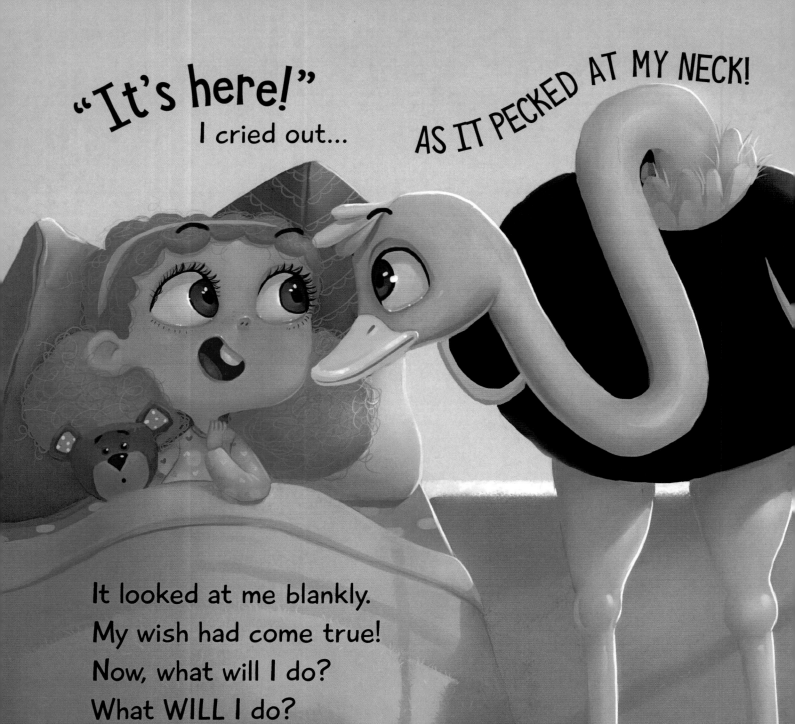

"Breakfast!" I pondered. "Now, what do you eat?

Spaghetti?

Hmmm...
marshmallows?

Popcorn?

Meat?"

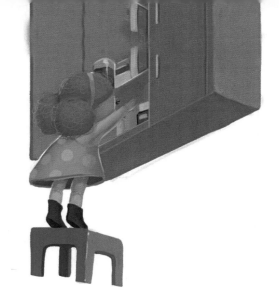

His appetite —
        as you've probably guessed,
had me running to find
        more for him to digest.

"Apples!" I cheered,
while collecting them all.

Then I carefully stacked
   them because he's so tall.
I sat in my chair
   to observe and to wait,

as he scarfed down the apples...

I called up the vet, Dr. Wally Kazoo,

"The apples are STUCK, Doctor!
What should I do?"

"Oh no!" Dr. Wally Kazoo said in shock,
"Go get him some butter —
a BIG, one-pound block."

"The apples will smoothly go down his long throat. This has worked for a monkey — a pig — and a goat."

I shoved all the butter right into his beak.
And the apples went down as I snuck in to peek.

Hmmm, what next?

I know!

An ostrich is active.
We'll get some fresh air.
What a beautiful day.
We can go anywhere!

An ostrich might like a
calm stroll at the zoo,
or maybe instead some
light jogging will do!

So, I put on his leash...

And he ran out the door!

Then behind him, I flew...

"Boy, this pet is a chore!"

But he just wouldn't listen although I was pleading.
He carried on running. 'Til soon, he was speeding.

I chased him right past a GIRAFFE

and RACCOON.

And on past a HIPPO

and then a BABOON.

I finally caught him.
I captured him quick,
but I was exhausted.

This ostrich was SLICK.

"I know where to take you," I said with a smile.
"We'll go to the beach, and we'll stay for a while."

"I think you just need a
nice calm place to play.
We can go for a swim and
build castles all day."

But instead, he just PLANTED his head in the sand.
I couldn't believe it. It's NOT what I'd planned.

He lifted his head and was running again! **THAT'S IT!**

"An ostrich," I thought, "cannot run in a home.

He must be in nature to romp and to roam."

So, I wished on a star shooting off in the night,
and wished at that moment with all of my might.

*Oh star, shining star, make my wishes come true,
please take my pet ostrich right back to the zoo.*

*Please send him away with his long, skinny neck,
please send him right back with that beak that will peck.*

The very next morning,
    I stretched with a yawn.
My wish had come true;
    my pet ostrich was gone!

As I dressed, I decided,
    "It's all for the best.
Because now I have time
    for my NEXT special guest."

I'll visit my friend at the big City Zoo.
I'll bring him some apples,
but only a few...

Then, I'll wish on a star, shooting off in the night...

I'll wish for a UNICORN with all of my might!!

Let's Have Some Fun
Learning What You Have Read!

⭐ Can you go back to the story and find words that rhyme?

⭐ How many animals can you find in the story?

⭐ What got "stuck" in the throat of the ostrich? What did the little girl give the ostrich to make him better?

⭐ How many apples did the ostrich eat?

⭐ What pet does the teacher have in the story?

⭐ What part of the story was your favorite? Why?

⭐ What did the little girl wish for at the end of the story?

⭐ If you could make a magical wish for a pet, what would it be? Draw a picture with a description and ask an adult to share it with me!

Dear Reader,

I hope you enjoyed reading this fun and silly book as much as I had enjoyed writing it. If this book brought a big smile to your face, please take a moment to leave an honest review on Amazon. I also enjoy seeing pictures of my readers too. Do not forget to send me your artwork and description of your magical wish for a pet!

Keep reading and I look forward to hearing from you!

xo,
Sarina

Check out the FREE activity pages and be the first to know about new book releases at www.sarinasiebenaler.com

Sarina is also available to connect with you for an author visit. Details are located at the aforementioned website, or you may contact her at books@sarinasiebenaler.com

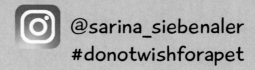 @sarina_siebenaler
#donotwishforapet

About the Author

Sarina Siebenaler is an author, autism advocate, mom of three children and one dog. She writes children's books to encourage literacy, spark a child's imagination and to help with social and emotional skills. Her free time is spent running, hiking and traveling to new adventures with her family.